Nola The Nurse

She's On The Go Series Vol. 1

By Dr. Scharmaine L. Baker NP

Illustrated By Jasmine Mills

A DrNurse Publishing House
New Orleans, Louisiana

Nola The Nurse™ She's On The Go series Vol. 1
Text copyright © 2015 by Scharmaine Lawson-Baker
Illustrations copyright © Scharmaine Lawson-Baker

2475 Canal Street, Suite 240, new Orleans, La. 70119
www.NolatheNurse.com

ISBN 978-0-9912407-1-5

Author Contact info:
info@DrBakerNP.com
@NolaTheNurse
@DrBakerNP
www.DrBakerNP.com
www.NolaTheNurse.com

To Whitney, Skylar, and Wyatt.

Thanks for allowing mommy to be creative and moody.

~Schar

"Keep still, Gumbo," Nola said to her puppy.

Nola wanted to be a nurse practitioner like her mother. She knew how to check temperatures and bandage cuts and bruises because she saw how her mother cared for her patients.

He jumped up and ran off with the bandage dragging on the ground behind him.

"Come back, Gumbo!" little Nola yelled as she chased after him.

She bumped into her mother in the dining room

"Trying to play nurse again, Nola?" her mother asked. She was wearing her nurse practitioner's outfit. She was going to work.

"Yes, Mommy, and Gumbo won't sit still so I can put a bandage on his leg." Nola sighed.

"Tell you what, Nola, let's have some lunch. Then you can come with me to visit some patients. We can come back later and chase Gumbo."

Nola liked going to work with her mother. Sometimes they went to the hospital. There she could watch as the nurse practitioners and physicians went around looking after sick people. They were trying to make them better. When she grew up she wanted to be a nurse practitioner just like her mommy.

Today, they were going to visit sick people in their homes. The first house they went to was where Ms. Aleta lived.

"Hello, Ms. Aleta. How are you today?" her mother asked.

"Still having some pains in my legs," the old lady said. "I see you've brought your little one with you." She smiled at Nola.

"Yes. Say hello to Ms. Aleta, dear."

"Hello. My name is Nola, and when I grow up, I want to be a nurse practitioner just like my mommy."

"Oh, that's very good," said Ms. Aleta.

Nola watched as her mother took Ms. Aleta's temperature, listened to her heart beat and gave her a prescription.

"You'll be fine, Ms. Aleta. Don't you worry," Nola's mother said.

Nola and her mother visited three more sick people before they went back home.

"Can I go outside and play, Mommy?" Nola asked.

"Yes, dear. But stay on the sidewalk."

"I will."

Nola went into her room. She put on her nurse's uniform that her mother had bought her. She then picked up her little nurse practitioner kit. She was ready to play nurse practitioner.

She went into the garage, got onto her bike, and rode out onto the sidewalk.

Ring! Ring! Ring! She rang the bell as she rode around the neighborhood while being careful to remain on the sidewalk, just as mommy had asked.

"Here come's Nola," said Ellen, her friend from across the street.

Nola smiled. She liked being called a nurse practitioner. All of her friends knew that she liked playing a nurse practitioner, and they always let her look after their dolls.

"Are there any sick dolls to look after today?" Nola asked.

"Oh yes," said Ellen. "Mia has a tummy ache. Won't you come and see her?"

Nola went into the house. Mia, Ellen's doll, was lying on the bed.

Just like she saw her mother do, Nola looked after the doll. She took care of her by taking her temperature, listening to her heartbeat and giving her a prescription.

"She'll be fine," Nola said.

Nola liked to help during emergencies. At the hospital, everybody rushed around doing many things to help the sick people. Now she could pretend to be doing just that. She, Ellen, and Shani rushed outside to the next house.

Mrs. Choge, Shani's mother, met them at the door. "Hello, Ellen and Nola. Don't tell me. You've come to look after one of Shani's sick dolls. Right?"

"How did you know, Mrs. Choge?" Nola asked.

"Well, I see you have your nurse practitioner kit in your hand, and you have on your nurse outfit."

Nola smiled. Everyone knew that she was a nurse practitioner.

"Hurry, Nola, Dali, my doll, is crying."

Nola hurried into the room. Ellen and Shani watched as she wiped the doll's knee with a tissue before putting on a Band-Aid.

Nola always washed her hands with lots of soap and bubbles after treating her dolls. She loved washing those germs away. Always wash your hands, everyday.

When Nola was done, just like her mother, she said to Shani, "Dali will be fine. Don't you worry." "Thank you, Nola. You saved my doll's life," said Shani.

The three of them laughed. Nola always had fun playing nurse practitioner with her friends.

As Nola got ready to leave, Mrs. Choge came into the room. "We are just about to have something to eat. Why don't you all have some? I'm sure your mothers won't mind."

This was true. Their families were all friends, and the children went from one house to the other all the time.

Ellen, Shani, and Nola went into the dining room, where Mrs. Choge gave them some stew and spaghetti. The stew tasted sweet and tangy.

"What is this, Mrs. Choge?" Nola asked. She had never tasted anything like it before.

"You mean the stew? It's something we call matoke. We eat it a lot in Kenya where I come from. We make it from plantains, meat, tomatoes and other ingredients."

Nola went home with a full tummy, and she was feeling very happy. She'd had a good time playing a nurse practitioner, and she had eaten some delicious Kenyan food.

Matoke Recipe

1 hr 20 min - 468.7 cal

Ingredients:

Plantains or green bananas (see notes), peeled and diced -- 6 to 8
Lemon, juice only -- 1
Oil -- 2 to 3 tablespoons
Onion, chopped -- 1
Bell pepper, chopped -- 1
Garlic, minced -- 3 or 4 cloves
Chile peppers, finely chopped -- 3 or 4
Ground coriander -- 1 tablespoon
Stewing beef (optional), cubed -- 1 pound
Tomatoes, seeded and chopped -- 2 cups
Water or beef stock -- 2 cups
Salt -- to season

Method:

Toss the plantains with the lemon juice and set aside.

Heat the oil in a large pot over medium-high flame. Add the onions and bell pepper and saute until the onion is cooked through and translucent, about 3 or 4 minutes. Add the garlic, chile peppers and coriander and saute for another minute or so.

Stir in the beef and tomatoes and cook for another 2 or 3 minutes.

Add the beef stock or water and season with salt. Bring to a boil, then reduce heat to medium-low, cover and simmer for about 20 minutes.

Stir in the plantains and simmer for another 30 to 40 minutes, or until the beef is tender and the plantains have softened. Adjust seasoning and serve hot.

Matoke Variations:

Meat: Try using goat or lamb meat instead of beef. Brown the meat in the oil first for a deeper flavor, then add the onions and peppers. You can also use ground beef.

Dried Fish: Authentic matoke often includes

dried, smoked fish. Take a piece of dried fish, usually catfish, and soak it until it is tender. Then debone the fish and flake it. Stir it into the stew along with the beef and tomatoes.

Vegetarian Matoke: Matoke is just as tasty when served as a vegetarian meal. Simply eliminate the beef and use water or vegetable stock.

Peanut-Flavored Matoke: Stir in 1/4 to 1/2 cup of natural peanut butter or finely chopped peanuts during the last 5 minutes of cooking.

Recipe courtesy of www.whats4eats.com

What is a Nurse Practitioner?

All nurse practitioners (NPs) must complete a master's or doctoral degree program, and have advanced clinical training beyond their initial professional registered nurse preparation. Didactic and clinical courses prepare nurses with specialized knowledge and clinical competency to practice in primary care, acute care and long-term health care settings.

To be recognized as expert health care providers and ensure the highest quality of care, NPs undergo rigorous national certification, periodic peer review, clinical outcome evaluations, and adhere to a code for ethical practices. Self-directed continued learning and professional development is also essential to maintaining clinical competency.

Additionally, to promote quality health care and improve clinical outcomes, NPs lead and participate in both professional and lay health care forums, conduct research and apply findings to clinical practice.

NPs are licensed in all states and the District of Columbia, and practice under the rules and regulations of the state in which they are licensed. They provide high-quality care in rural, urban and suburban communities, in many types of settings including clinics, hospitals, emergency rooms, urgent care sites, private physician or NP practices, nursing homes, schools, colleges, and public health departments.

What sets NPs apart from other health care providers is their unique emphasis on the health and well-being of the whole person. With a focus on health promotion, disease prevention, and health education and counseling, NPs guide patients in making smarter health and lifestyle choices, which in turn can lower patients' out-of-pocket costs.

American Association of Nurse Practitioners, 2015
www.AANP.org

Four Star Review

Reviewed by Micaela Alpert for Readers' Favorite

Nola the Nurse: She's On The Go by Dr. Scharmaine L Baker is about a little girl Nola, and her adventures with her mother, who is a nurse. In the beginning of the story, Nola is playing with her dog and trying to out bandages on him. She is playing nurse. Her mother is a nurse, so Nola decides to let her dog be, and follow her mom around while her mom helps sick people. Today, Nola is going with her mom to people's homes, and helping people who can't be transported to the hospital. After several of those visits, Nola decides to go home and play nurse to fix all her friends' dolls up.

Nola the Nurse is a great book for young children to read, even those who don't know what they want to be when they grow up. Young children will definitely like this story, and I hope this book ends up in children's bookstores and many schools. This book has a picture on every other page, which will attract a little one's attention and stop them from losing interest in this book. I really liked this book because Dr. Baker wrote it to be culturally sensitive to African-American nurses, which is also why it is a great book for young children because teaching them to be culturally sensitive at a young age is very important. I believe that this book has many reasons why it is great, and I hope that young readers think so too.

About the Author

Dr. Lawson-Baker received her DNP in 2008 from Chatham University. In 2004, after 20 years of nursing, she opened the first NP Housecall practice in the state of Louisiana. In 2008, she was awarded the ADVANCE for Nurse Practitioner magazine's esteemed Entrepreneur of the Year award and was featured on the cover of the journal. She was also interviewed by Katie Couric on CBS Evening News for her innovative ways to improve access to healthcare especially after Hurricane KATRINA. Highly sought after for keynote speaking and countless other media venues, she is the CEO of Advanced Clinical Consultants and owner of The Housecall Course which is the only course in the nation training NPs on how to start a Housecall practice. Her most recent accomplishments are the 2013 New Orleans City Business Healthcare Hero award and establishing a publishing company entitled: A DrNurse Publishing House for all of her literary work. Dr. Baker is extremely excited about her children's book series entitled: Nola the Nurse which was debuted in May, 2015. More fiction and non-fiction books are slated to be released in 2015.

CPSIA information can be obtained at www.ICGtesting.com
Printed in the USA
BVIW12n0712190717
489687BV00003B/55